This Book Belongs To

Today was Mom's birthday and Jamaal wanted to do something special. He decided that he would bake a birthday cake for her. Of course, his best friend Gizmo would help. They would have fun baking the cake together. Dad said that it would be a good idea and he would be there to help if needed.

Jamaal began to prepare the birthday cake. He looked in the kitchen cupboard for a box of cake mix. Gizmo climbed into the cupboard to help him find it. They also found a box of icing sugar to decorate the cake and some candles to put on the top.

Once they got everything together, Jamaal began to read the directions on the box of cake mix. Because Gizmo had never seen a birthday cake, he did not know how to help. Jamaal had to show him what he could do. They both tried their best to make it the best birthday cake ever.

When the cake was baked, they began to decorate it. Jamaal mixed the icing and Gizmo helped by tasting it to make sure it was sweet enough. When Jamaal and Gizmo finished decorating the cake, they put candles on it. Jamaal thought it was the best one he had ever seen. He knew Mom would be happy.

That evening when Mom came home, Jamaal and Gizmo showed her the birthday cake they had baked to help them all to celebrate her birthday. Mom told them that she was very happy, and that this was her best birthday ever! Jamaal and Gizmo were very happy to celebrate Mom's birthday.

Stars and Moonbeams and Boundless Dreams. That's What Little Boys Are Made of.
                                                    -Jim Brown